INDIANA JONES™

and the

KINGDOM OF
THE CRYSTAL SKULL™

Movie Storybook

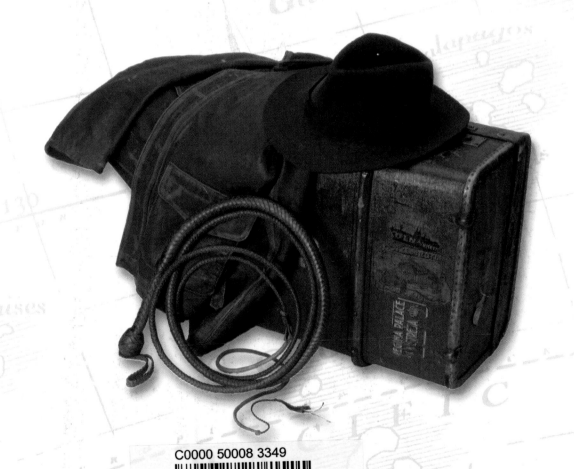

Indiana Jones and the Kingdom of the Crystal Skull

First published in Great Britain by HarperCollins Children's Books in 2008
1 3 5 7 9 10 8 6 4 2

ISBN 13: 978-0-00-727782-7
ISBN 10: 0-00-727782-2

Printed in Italy by Rotolito Lombarda

HarperCollins *Children's Books*

INDIANA JONES

and the

KINGDOM OF
THE CRYSTAL SKULL

Story by
George Lucas and Jeff Nathanson

Screenplay by
David Koepp

Dr. Indiana Jones and his friend Mac have been kidnapped by Russian spies and taken to a top-secret military base. There, he was forced to aid the Russians while they searched a huge hangar for a small, magnetized crate.

Once Indy had found the crate for the Russians, they opened it. Inside was a metallic body bag – and inside that was what looked like an alien!

Indy tried to escape the Russians. He grabbed his bullwhip and a gun from one of the spies, but his friend, Mac, it turned out, was working for the enemy. He and the Russians forced Indy to drop his gun. Not about to give up, he tossed the gun in the air – it landed and fired!

As Indy scrambled over some crates to escape, the leader of the Russians, Dr. Irina Spalko, ordered the alien body onto a jeep – they were taking it away.

Indy chased after the Russians, causing a few crashes as jeeps and crates collided in the huge hangar's maze of top-secret treasures. A jeep screeched in front of him, tossing them down a flight of stairs.

Indy saw train tracks that led into a dark tunnel. A Russian named Dovchenko threw him onto railroad flat car with a huge jet engine attached to it. Indy saw Mac and more soldiers running down the stairs toward them – he had to act fast!

Indy kicked the jet engine's throttle and it burst to life, shooting the flat car down the tracks, out of the bunker and into the desert. By the time the engine finally slowed to a halt, Dovchenko had passed out, but Indy saw more Russians approaching. He made for the hills.

Dr. Spalko had stored the alien in a getaway car. She had followed the tracks, and ordered soldiers to follow the pair of footprints that led off into the distance.

Indy came to a strange, deserted town. He spotted some Russians down the street in a jeep, so he ran into a house.

Inside, he thought he had found some people – but they turned out to be mannequins. Back outside, he saw a sign that read, "U.S. Nevada Proving Ground. CIVILIANS TURN BACK." Then he saw a nuclear bomb suspended from a platform. The Russians, who had caught up with him, saw it, too – and they sped off in their cars without him! "Sure, don't bother to wait for me," Indiana laughed.

"T-minus thirty seconds and counting," an ominous voice boomed over loudspeakers.

Indy ran back into the house and looked for something to hide in for protection – the refrigerator! Lead-lined for superior insulation, a sign read inside the door. Perfect! Indy threw himself inside. As the door closed, the bomb exploded.

The blast shot the refrigerator far from the town. After it finally came to a stop, Indy managed to get the door open. Stumbling out of the refrigerator, he looked back to see a huge mushroom cloud in the distance.

Indy was rescued by an Army patrol and taken to a decontamination room, where everything checked out. He was okay.

Two men in black suits questioned him about what happened. As the two continued questioning Indy, his friend General Robert Ross entered the room. He told Professor Jones that Dr. Irina Spalko was a top Russian scientist who was searching the world for artifacts that might have military uses. She carried a case of deadly swords with her.

"Some things never change," Indy replied.

Back home, Indy packed for a trip and was going to take a train bound for New York City. As the train departed, a kid in a leather jacket came racing onto the platform on his motorcycle.

"Hey, mister! Hey, buddy! Hey, professor!" the kid shouted at Indy, keeping up with the departing train, which was about to enter a tunnel. "You're an old friend of Harold Oxley, right?"

"What about him?" Indy replied.

"They're gonna kill him!" the kid said, braking as the train went into the tunnel.

The kid thought Indy was gone. Then Dr. Jones appeared, suitcase in hand.

But neither one of them saw the men who were following them.

Indy and the kid went to Arnie's diner, which was packed with college students. The kid, whose name was Mutt Williams, told Indy that Oxley, or Ox as they called him, had gone in search of a crystal skull in Peru.

The crystal skull interested Indy. "Stare into the eyes of the skull and learn the secrets of the universe," Indy said. "Or maybe go mad."

"Ox said he found one in Peru," Mutt replied, "and that he was bringing it to a place called Akator."

Indiana Jones explained that Akator was a lost city built about 7,000 years ago, a city of gold. In 1546, a conquistador named Francesco de Orellana had disappeared while looking for it. "Why would Ox want to take the skull there?" Mutt asked.

"It's believed in parts of South America that whoever finds the skull and returns it to Akator's temple will be granted control over its power," Indy replied.

Mutt's mother had gone to Peru to find Ox – she thought he'd gone crazy.

Then Mutt's mom had called him – both she and Ox had been kidnapped. Ox had hidden the skull, and if he didn't tell them where it was, the kidnappers said that either she or Ox was going to die.

"Who's your mom, kid?" Indy asked. Mutt said her name was Mary Williams. She had mailed Mutt a letter Ox had written, and on the phone had asked him to give it to Indy. She said he would help. Then the line went dead.

"It's complete gibberish," Mutt said, handing Indy the letter.

Indy didn't have time to respond. The two men who had followed him asked Professor Jones to come with them, and to bring the letter.

He and Mutt got up to leave, the thugs behind them.

"Mutt," Indy whispered. "Punch the prep in the face." Mutt understood Indy needed to cause a diversion so they could escape, and hit a boy standing next to him right in the jaw. All the kids in the diner started screaming and a riot broke out.

Indy and Mutt ran out into an alley where Mutt's motorcycle was.

"Your mom didn't escape, kid," Indy yelled over the engine's roar. "They let her go. They wanted her to mail Ox's letter, and they wanted you to bring that letter to me. Now they want me to translate it, and they plan on using you to make me do it!"

With that, Mutt and Indy raced away, a black sedan following close behind.

They zigzagged through the town's traffic – but after evading the first car, a second one caught up with them.

They zoomed down the streets and through the college library, thinking many times that they had lost the Russians, only to find the sedan on their tail again.

Finally, Mutt raced onto an access ramp, straight into a stadium where a football game was in progress!

The crowd yelled as Mutt and Indy raced down the centre of the field, and were even more startled when the Russians' sedan came crashing through a wooden fence and chased the bike!

Finally they were able to lose their pursuer.

Indy and Mutt snuck into Indy's house. Indy needed to consult some books to decode Ox's letter, which was written in an ancient South American language.

"So what are you, like 80?" Mutt joked as Indy translated.

Indy laughed, then read his translation: "Follow lines in the earth only gods can read to Orellana's cradle, guarded by the living dead."

Indy knew Ox was talking about the Nazca Lines – ancient pictures carved into the ground that were so huge they could be seen complete only from the sky. "Oxley's telling us the skull is somewhere in Nazca, Peru," he said.

The Russians had to be searching for the skull because of the psychic powers it gives whoever discovers Akator. He had to find it first.

Indiana Jones grabbed his whip and started packing.

Indy and Mutt made their way to New York City. There, they caught a plane to Mexico City. They spent the afternoon visiting ruins before boarding a plane that ultimately took them to Lima, Peru.

In Lima, Indy found them passage on a cargo plane that was flying to the Peruvian city of Arequipa. For a fee, the pilot agreed to drop them off at a small desert airstrip at Nazca.

Before they landed, the pilot flew them over the fabled Nazca Lines Oxley had written about in his coded message.

Mutt was bored for the first few days in Nazca. He found the food to be inedible and the dust made it hard for him to ride his cycle, which he had brought with him.

"Finally," Indy said, approaching Mutt with two locals after days of searching. "They say they remember Ox."

A couple of months before, Professor Oxley had staggered into town talking like a crazy person, so the local police had taken him to an asylum on the edge of town.

On the way to the asylum, Indy and Mutt talked. Mutt had dropped out of prep school – the only thing he'd enjoyed was his fencing class. Mutt wanted more than anything to be a motorcycle mechanic. Indy told him there was nothing wrong with that.

"And don't let anybody tell you different," Indy added.

A nun greeted Indy and Mutt when they arrived at the asylum.

"We're looking for an American named Harold Oxley," Indy explained.

"Men came and stole him away," the nun replied. "Men with guns."

Indy asked the nun if he and Mutt could see Oxley's cell, and she led them down a long, dark corridor, with eerie beams of light shining through small windows.

The nun brought them to Oxley's cell – it was dark and the floor was covered with sand.

"The lines only the gods can read," Indy said, reading Ox's letter aloud. "Leading to Orellana's cradle." How could the Nazca Lines lead them to Orellana?

Ox had drawn skulls all over his cell. He had also written the word "return" in many different languages. Then Indy noticed something under the sand. He ran out of the cell and grabbed a broom.

"Sweep!" he said, handing the broom to Mutt.

Standing on some stairs in the cell, as Mutt swept away the dust, Indy could start to make out a drawing on the ground of a graveyard next to the Nazca lines. Indy knew that Oxley had found Orellana! And Orellana was buried in this cemetery.

Mutt and Indy rode Mutt's motorcycle up to the cemetery, which stood on a ledge a hill above the town and above the Nazca lines.

Indy and Mutt passed through the creaky iron gate and saw gravestones, vaults, and mausoleums. Many of the graves had been robbed and skeletons had been thrown all over the grounds. They walked through the cemetery, searching for clues.

All of a sudden, two warriors jumped out of the darkness and attacked them! One lunged at Mutt and another came at Indy. Indy pulled out his whip and snapped it at the attackers as they battled.

The two guardians of the dead fought hard, but Indy and Mutt finally won.

Indy and Mutt then walked inside a cavern and found a carved stone wall that looked like a dead end. A skull was carved into the stone. It looked like it was breathing – there was air coming from the other side!

Indy stuck his fingers into the hollowed-out eyes of the skull and pulled. The skull came loose and he saw there was was a rope behind it. With a tug on the rope, the wall parted – to reveal a passageway behind it! As Mutt followed Indy into the secret passage, the floor started to give way – he was falling through the ledge of the hill! Indy pulled him out and warned him to be careful.

"Thanks for the advice," Mutt said as they walked down a staircase to a small chamber.

After passing through a tunnel, they came to another room. Seven bodies were wrapped in metallic foil. Indy pulled the foil of one back to reveal a Spanish conquistador. They had found Orellana and his men! They were perfectly preserved even though they were over 500 years old.

Indy had begun searching the bodies, peeling back the foil, when Mutt called him over – one had already been opened!

A gold mask had been placed over the head. "Francisco de Orellana himself," Indy exclaimed. Indy lifted the body up and reached behind it. He pulled out a gleaming crystal skull.

"Ox must have found it here and returned it for some reason," Indy told Mutt.

"Return," Mutt said, thinking of what Ox had written in his cell. Looking over, he saw Orellana's skeleton reaching out for the skull!

"It's not the arm," Indy said, looking over. "It's the armour." The skull was magnetic! The two stared at it, wondering what it really was.

As they continued to stare, they fell into a trance. Light showed in the skull's eyes and kept getting brighter. As they kept looking at the skull, the floor started to give way – the two raced back out of the passageway as huge chunks of floor fell out beneath them.

When they finally got out of the burial chamber, dawn was breaking.

"Hello, old pal," Indy heard as he was brushing off the dust.

It was Mac. The Russians were with him – there was no escape.

"Here we go again," Indy said, before he and Mutt were knocked out.

He had been kidnapped once more and didn't know where they were being taken. When he finally came to, he was inside a large tent tied to a chair. The air was really thick and humid.

Indy knew he was in the Amazonian jungle.

The sinister Dr. Irina Spalko entered the tent.

"You survive to be of service once again," Spalko said to Indy.

"You know me, anything I can do to help," he shot back.

Spalko told Indy her plan for the crystal skull – the Soviet Union was planning to use its psychic powers as a weapon against the United States!

"The skull is a mind weapon," Spalko said. She told Indy it was not made by the hands of man.

"Then whose hands made it?" Indy asked. With that, Spalko nodded to the object they had stolen from the hangar – the box containing the alien body!

"Saucer-men from Mars?" Indy said jokingly.

"The legends about Akator are true, Dr. Jones," Spalko snapped. "The skull was stolen from Akator in the fifteenth century. Whoever returns it…"

"To the city's temple gets control over its power," Indy interrupted. "But what if Akator doesn't exist?"

"You should ask your friend that question," Spalko said. "We're certain Professor Oxley has been there."

"Ox is here?" Indy said, trying to get untied.

When Indy saw Oxley, the professor was babbling insanely. "Through eyes that I last saw in tears," he said, over and over again. His right hand was twitching.

Mac told Indy the crystal skull had made Oxley crazy.

"Henry Jones Junior!" Ox said over and over again.

"He is a divining rod that will lead us to Akator," Spalko added. "You will help him remember the way to Akator." With that, Dovchenko strapped Indy to a chair and the crystal skull was placed in front of him.

The skull began to pulsate and Indy was transfixed. All the while, Spalko told of her plan to use the skull to control the thoughts of entire populations.

Indy was hypnotized. He stared at the skull and said, "Return."

Convinced that Indy was under the skull's spell, Spalko ordered him brought together with Oxley. Indy hadn't stared at the skull as long as Oxley had and would be able to translate Oxley's gibberish. Indy refused to help them and they dragged him from the tent.

Outside the tent, Indy saw Mutt. Spalko drew a sword and threatened Mutt's life. "Don't give these Reds a thing," Mutt said to Indy.

Spalko decided to persuade Indy in a different way and barked orders at two Russian soldiers.

"Take your hands off me!" Indy heard a familiar voice yell – Marion Ravenwood! They had found the Ark of the Covenant together many years ago. They had been in love, but it hadn't worked out. What was she doing here?

"Marion!" Indy yelled.

"Well, it's about time you showed up, Jones," she said.

"Mom!" Mutt called.

Indy was shocked. "Marion Ravenwood is your mother?" He stammered.

Indy couldn't believe he was with Marion again, or that he had been with her son searching for Oxley. Marion was just as beautiful as he remembered, and just as feisty.

Spalko raised the sword again – this time to Marion's throat.

"Perhaps you will help us now, Dr. Jones," she said. "A simple 'yes' will suffice."

Indy approached Oxley. Ox repeated several quotations, none of which Indy could understand. Finally, Indy asked for some paper – Ox wanted to write something. That was why his hand was twitching.

"Three times it drops," Ox said as he hurriedly drew pages of symbols. Indy stared at the symbols. He finally got it! Ox was drawing directions to Akator!

"Map!" Indy yelled. He pieced together Ox's directions – where the Sono River joined the Amazon, there was an expanse of uncharted land. It had to be there!

As Spalko and Dovchenko leaned over the map for a closer look, Mutt knocked them over.

"Run!" he shouted to Indy, Marion, and Oxley as he scrambled away from the camp.

"Kid, hold up," Indy shouted to Mutt after they had run through the jungle for quite a while. Indy and Mutt began arguing over what to do next.

"Mutt," Marion said, trying to calm him down. She was about to say something else when she felt herself sinking into the ground. She looked down – she and Indy were both sinking into the fine sand! Mutt ran off to find something to help pull them out. They were sinking fast.

"Ox," Indy said. "Are you gonna help us?" Ox turned and wandered off into the jungle.

"About Mutt, Indy," Marion said, thinking she was about to die, stumbling on her words. "His name is Henry."

"Henry? How could you do that to him?" Indy yelled.

"Because he's your son, Indy," Marion confessed. "Henry Jones the third."

Before they could continue, Mutt burst from the jungle and threw something into the sand. "Grab hold of it!" he yelled. "I'll pull you out!"

Indy screamed. "It's a snake!" Indy hated snakes. Marion yelled at him to grab it and so did Mutt. Finally, he complied and Mutt dragged them from the sand pit.

As the snake was slithering away from them, Ox appeared.

"I brought help," he said. With that, Mac and the Russians appeared.

Indy, Marion, Mutt, and Oxley were in the last truck of a convoy chopping its way through the rainforest. At the front of the line was a giant mulcher, crunching any tree that got in its way, clearing a path for the rest of the trucks.

"You've got to be kidding me!" Mutt yelled. Marion told Mutt that Indy was his father. He had always thought his father was a British RAF pilot. He was wrong.

Indy and Marion were supposed to be married but Indy had left. He was afraid she wouldn't like being married to an adventurer. She had never told him about Mutt.

"So why'd you bother telling me now?" Indy asked.

"I thought we were dying!" she exclaimed.

Dovchenko had grown tired of listening to this, and was making gags to tie around their mouths. When he bent over, Indy kicked him toward Mutt, who kicked him again, knocking him out!

Indy commandeered the truck they were in. Marion and Mutt joined him in the front after he pushed the driver out.

"We have to get Oxley," Indy yelled. "Get our hands on that skull and get to Akator before Spalko does!" He told Marion to take the wheel.

"What's he going to do next?" Mutt asked, just as Indy pulled a bazooka from the back of the truck and aimed it at the mulcher. "You might want to cover your ears," he said before launching the rocket. It zoomed past the trucks – and scored a direct hit on the mulcher, which lurched to a halt. Half of the trucks in the convoy rammed into it, parts flying and smoke rising in the jungle.

"Jones!" Spalko seethed.

Indy, Marion, and Mutt leapt out of their truck and into a vehicle that could drive on land and in water called a "duck." Spalko jumped into a jeep with Dovchenko, and started blasting at them with a gun, firing at them as they weaved between other Russian cars in the convoy.

Marion drove alongside the truck Oxley and the skull were in. Indy jumped over to the truck and knocked the driver out of the way. Mac was in the cab and he decided to switch sides and keep the Russians off Indy. He told Indy he was a double-agent. As the two were fighting to keep control of the car, Spalko caught up with them and yelled for the soldier guarding Oxley to throw her the skull.

Now that she had it, she wanted revenge. She told the driver to get even with Indy's car. As he did so, she leaned toward Indy, swinging her sword at him.

As she was lashing her sword at Indy, she felt something – a blade. Someone was attacking her! She turned and saw Mutt swinging at her from the Duck. He had a foil. She defended herself and, from two separate vehicles, the two engaged in battle.

"You duel like a beginner," she snapped at Mutt, who knew she was right. He was working hard to fight and she was deflecting his strikes with ease.

As they drove on, the fight continued. The trucks hit a bump and Mutt was thrown into the back of Spalko's truck as she went flying into the back of the vehicle Marion was driving. Mutt saw the sack with the skull and lunged for it. He had it, but not for long – Spalko managed to return – and in one push, she knocked him from the truck and snatched the sack from him.

Mutt was stuck in the trees – but he swung on vines, one from the other, until he caught up with Spalko. He grabbed the sack from her and leapt into the vehicle Indy was driving. Oxley was there and he was safe – for the moment.

The chase came to a temporary stop in front of a huge mound. Army ants, disturbed when a truck slammed into their home, suddenly swarmed out of the anthill. Everyone scrambled, swatting the ants away.

Meanwhile, Marion, Indy, Ox, Mac, and Mutt had gotten into the Duck. They had driven to a dead end that looked out over the river. But Marion knew what she had to do – she drove straight for the edge of the cliff.

"Three times it drops," Oxley said as they drove over the cliff and onto an underlying tree.

Marion accelerated and the car fell again, landing in the choppy waters of the river. Mac activated the vehicle's water propellers and Marion manoeuvred the choppy waters of the river.

They fell down three waterfalls, one worse than the other, until they were finally thrown from the vehicle and into the river.

They had all crawled up onto the riverbank when they heard a strange sound. The pebbles were shaking all around them. Oxley had taken the skull out of its bag and turned it to face behind them. Indy turned around and saw in the mesa a giant head, a waterfall pouring out of one of its eyes.

"Akator?" Mutt asked.

"We've found it!" Indy shouted.

"Through eyes that last I saw in tears," Oxley said.

Mutt said, "That's the entrance – through the waterfall!"

"The skull has to be returned," Indy said, looking at the face of the kingdom of the crystal skull.

"Why you?" Marion asked, wondering why Indy had to take on such a task.

"Because it asked me to," he replied.

Up the mountain they climbed until they came to the eye. As they crawled through the waterfall, they saw on the tunnel's walls beautiful ancient murals. They stopped at one showing humans gazing up at a tall, glowing humanoid in the sky. The further they travelled, the more detailed the murals became. Indy found one image whose head matched the shape of the crystal skull exactly. Other panels showed thirteen of the beings in a circle, and a battle in which one of the beings had lost its head – the skull Oxley had found!

The final room contained thirteen huge skull sculptures. As the group was passing beneath them, they exploded – warriors poured out! Indy and the group ran.

They found the stairway that led down to Akator – the ruins of a huge city built in a crater. All around the city's edge, hills had been hollowed out to serve as a reservoir. The warriors followed them and more showed up. But Oxley took the skull out of the bag and held it up in the air facing the warriors. Strange beams shot out of its eyes. The warriors crept away in fear, as Oxley said, "Up," to Indy.

At the top they found a square basin filled with sand. Four obelisk parts were lying on their sides in the basin, and Oxley shook his head. This was as far as he had come when he had been here before. He hadn't solved the riddle of the obelisk.

"It's a puzzle," Indy said. "We have to reassemble the original obelisk." He saw plugs at the bottom of the basin. He grabbed a rock and smashed a plug out, sand pouring everywhere. Mac and Mutt joined in and the obelisk pieces levitated, finally forming one column.

The obelisk assembled, the group marveled for a moment before the structure began to open, revealing an inner portion with a stairway that ran down into an even more mysterious tunnel. As they scrambled down the stairs – the steps began to vanish! Beneath them were huge spikes with the skeletons of those who had fallen from the stairs. As fast as they could they ran down the remaining steps before they disappeared.

But all this time Indy and the others didn't realize that Spalko was following them – Mac had been dropping blinking diodes so she could stay on their trail.

The group with Indy came to two huge doors, which Indy opened after placing the skull in a niche. When they passed through the door, they saw thirteen seated crystal skeletons on thrones, one missing a head.

"Let me guess – the skull's his," Mutt said, as Spalko and her soldiers entered.

Indy couldn't believe Mac would do this to him... twice.

Spalko snatched the skull from Oxley and gazed at it. "Speak to me now," she said. She walked toward the headless being. "Imagine what they'll be able to tell us."

"I can't," Indy warned, "and neither can you."

Suddenly the skull flew from Spalko's hands and took its place on the being's shoulders. Indy and the others backed away.

Strange sounds arose from the being's body as the chamber walls began to crumble. The walls split – the building was falling apart.

Everyone but Spalko panicked as the beings began to come to life. The one whose head had been returned made a gesture to Oxley that it wanted to give him a gift for being made whole again.

"Tell me everything you know! I want it all," cried Spalko, entranced.

The last of the stones broke away and a whirlpool formed in the centre of the floor, sucking in the loose objects in the room.

"What is that thing?" Marion screamed.

"A portal," said Oxley, who had been released from his strange trance. "A pathway." It was a door to another dimension!

Indy suggested that they run before they were sucked into the whirlpool.

Indy, Marion, Oxley, Mutt, and Mac scrambled out of the room. The entire city was collapsing and water was pouring in from the aqueduct.

But Spalko was transfixed by the thirteen beings, as the whirlpool drew closer and closer to her. "I can see it all!" she was screaming, the knowledge of the universe destroying her mind. One by one, the beings vanished into another dimension, and she crumpled to the floor.

The group was rushing out when Mac got caught in the whirlpool – he had stolen jewels from the kingdom, and their weight and magnetism was slowing him down. Indy tried to help him, but the pull was too strong and Indy had to let go.

As the water rushed through, they found a tunnel and saw sunlight coming through it. As they scrambled into it, the increasing water pressure shot them up and out onto a grassy slope.

When they turned and looked, the entire kingdom was underwater – there was no trace it had ever existed.

Indy was standing in a new suit and bowtie. Next to him stood Marion, looking beautiful in a simple dress-suit. Mutt stood behind his father as the minister started the wedding ceremony.

Indy suddenly pulled Marion to him and kissed her.

"Well done, Henry!" Ox shouted as many guests cheered.

"Thanks, Ox," Indy said, pulling Marion close to him again.

He had found what he was looking for at Akator.

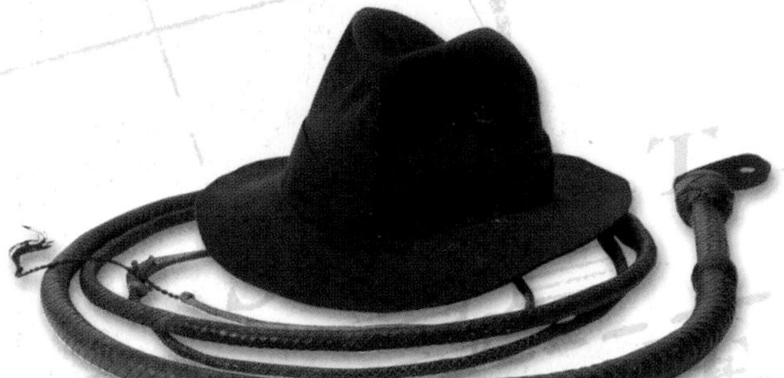